THE
LION KING

PaRragon

Bath New York Singapore Hong Kong Cologne Delhi Melbourne

Welcome to the Pride Lands, home to some of the most glorious animals in Africa. I am Rafiki, and I am here to tell you the story of one special lion that lives here – a lion that holds a very dear place in my heart. You can read along with me in your book. Every time you hear this sound...

you will know it is time to turn the page Let us begin now.

Every morning, as the sun peeks over the horizon, a giant rock formation catches the first rays of light. This is Pride Rock, home to my good friend King Mufasa and his lovely wife, Queen Sarabi. On this particular morning, animals from all over the Pride Lands had journeyed to Pride Rock to honour the birth of their newborn cub, Simba.

As part of the celebration, I had a special duty. I cracked open a gourd, dipped my finger inside, and made a mark on Simba's forehead. Then I lifted the future king up high for all to see. The elephants trumpeted with their trunks, the monkeys jumped up and down and the zebras stamped their hooves with happiness.

Not far from the ceremony, in a cave at the backside of Pride Rock, a scraggly lion with a dark mane grumbled. "Life's not fair. I shall never be king". This was Mufasa's brother, Scar, who was jealous of Simba's position as the next king.

Moments later, Mufasa was at the doorway to the cave. "Sarabi and I didn't see you at the presentation of Simba".

Zazu, Mufasa's trusted advisor, also appeared. " You should have been first in line."

"I was first in line until the little hairball was born." And with that, Scar stalked out of the cave.

Before long, Simba grew into a healthy, playful young cub. Early one morning, he and Mufasa climbed to the top of Pride Rock. As they looked out at the rising sun, Mufasa pointed to the light beams that stretched across the Pride Lands. "Look Simba: Everything the light touches is our kingdom."

Simba scanned the horizon and noticed a dark spot in the distance. "What about that shadowy place?"

"That's beyond our borders. You must never go there, Simba."

"But I thought a king can do whatever he wants."

"There's more to being king than getting your way all the time. Everything you see exists together in a delicate balance. As king you need to understand that balance and respect all the creatures – from the crawling ant to the leaping antelope. We are all connected in the great Circle of Life."

Later, as Simba headed back down the path, he ran into Scar. "Hey, Uncle Scar! Guess what? I'm gonna be king of Pride Rock. My dad just showed me the whole kingdom! And I'm gonna rule it all!"

Scar looked slyly at the young cub. "He didn't show you what's beyond that rise of the northern border."

"Well, no. He said I can't go there."

"And he's absolutely right. It's far too dangerous. Only the bravest lions go there. Promise me you'll never visit that dreadful place."

When Simba returned home, he found his friend Nala and her mother, Sarafina, visiting with Sarabi. "Come on! I just heard about this great place!"

The mothers gave permission for the youngsters to go, as long as Zazu went with them. Simba and Nala raced across the Pride Lands in an effort to lose the watchful bird. They led him through many herds of animals until they finally lost him.

Once the cubs were free of Zazu, Simba pounced on Nala, then Nala flipped Simba onto his back. They tumbled down a hill and landed in a dark ravine littered with elephant skulls and bones.

Simba looked around and gasped. "This is it! We made it!"

Before the cubs could explore any further, Zazu tracked them down.

"We're way beyond the boundary of the Pride Lands. And right now we are all in very real danger."

Suddenly three hyenas slithered out of the eye sockets of an elephant skull. Frightened, Simba, Zazu and Nala jumped back. It was Banzai, his partner, Shenzi, and the always-laughing Ed.

Banzai sneered. "A trio of trespassers."

Zazu tried to lead the cubs to safety, but Banzai grabbed him by the neck and plopped him down. The hyenas circled their prey, licking their chops.

"What's the hurry? We'd love you to stick around for dinner."

While the hyenas argued about who was going to eat whom, Simba, Nala and Zazu quietly slipped away. But the hyenas weren't distracted for long. They gave chase, and Simba and Nala had to run as fast as they could. Finally they tried hiding behind some elephant bones.

Just when it looked as if it were all over for the young cubs, Mufasa appeared and sent the hyenas flying with a swipe of his big paw.

"If you ever come near my son again…"

The hyenas slinked away, and Mufasa glared at Simba. "You deliberately disobeyed me! I'm very disappointed in you!"

Mufasa sent Nala and Zazu home so he could talk privately to his son. Simba peered up at his father.

"I was just trying to be brave, like you."

"Being brave doesn't mean you go looking for trouble."

"Dad, we're pals, right? And we'll always be together, right?"

Mufasa looked up at the stars. "Simba, let me tell you something my father told me: Look at the stars. The great kings of the past look down on us from those stars. So whenever you feel alone, just remember that those kings will always be there to guide you. And so will I."

Meanwhile the hyenas received another visitor: An angry Scar showed up at their lair. "I practically gift-wrapped those cubs for you and you couldn't even dispose of them." Scar warned the hyenas to be prepared.

Banzai laughed. "Yeah! Be prepared. We'll be prepared!… For what?"

Scar looked at him with danger in his eyes. "For the death of the king."

The following day, Scar invited Simba to join him in the gorge. When they arrived, Scar turned to his young nephew. "Now you wait here. Your father has a marvelous surprise for you."

Moments after he left, Scar signalled the hyenas, who chased a herd of wildebeests directly toward Simba.

From a distance, Mufasa noticed the rising dust. Scar appeared quickly at his side. "Stampede! In the gorge! Simba's down there!"

Without waiting a second, Mufasa took off to save his young son.

Mufasa plunged into the gorge and battled his way through the oncoming wildebeests. He found Simba, grabbed him by the nape of his neck, and put him on a nearby ledge. Suddenly Mufasa was knocked back into the stampede. "Dad!"

Desperately he tried to climb up another ledge from which Scar stood looking down on him. "Brother-help me!"

Scar reached for Mufasa and pulled him close enough to whisper in his ear. "Long live the king." Then Scar let go of Mufasa and he fell to his death.

Simba peered over the ridge just as his father disappeared beneath the thundering stampede.

Later, Scar found Simba hovering over his father's body, sobbing. "It was an accident. I didn't mean for it to happen."

"But the king is dead. And if it weren't for you, he'd still be alive. Oh, what will your mother think?"

Simba sobbed harder. "What am I gonna do?"

"Run away, Simba. Run! Run away and never return."

Simba did as he was told, unaware that his uncle`s hyena friends had been ordered to finish him off. Scar returned to Pride Rock to take over the throne.

Meanwhile, Simba plodded across the savannah without any food or water. It wasn't long before he fainted under the hot sun.

As the vultures circled overhead, a big-hearted warthog named Pumbaa stumbled upon the young lion. He turned to his trusty pal, a fast-talking meerkat named Timon. "He's so cute and all alone. Can we keep him?"

"Pumbaa, are you nuts? Lions eat guys like us." But Pumbaa scooped Simba up anyway, and carried him to safety.

When Simba awoke, the first thought that sprang to mind was his father's death. Timon taught him about Hakuna Matata, which means no responsibilities, no worries.

"You gotta put your past behind you."

And that is exactly what Simba did. He stayed in the jungle with Pumbaa and Timon a long, long time, and grew into a very big lion. But eventually he got homesick. One night he looked up at the stars and recalled the words his father had told him long ago. "The great kings of the past look down on us from those stars. So whenever you feel alone, just remember that those kings will always be there to guide you. And so will I."

The next day, Pumbaa was stalked and chased by a lioness. Simba came to his rescue, but after wrestling with the lioness, who easily flipped him onto his back, he realized that she was his old friend.

"Nala? What are you doing here?"

"Why didn't you come back to Pride Rock? You're the king!"

"I'm not the king. Scar is."

"Simba, he let the hyenas take over the Pride Lands."

"What?"

"There's no food, no water. If you don't do something soon, everyone will starve. You're our only hope."

"I can't go back."

Simba yelled at the heavens. "You said you'd always be there for me, but you're not…because of me."

Simba didn't believe he could challenge Scar to the throne, so he stayed in the jungle with Nala and his new friends.

But I knew the time had come for Simba to take his place in the Circle of Life, and I headed for the jungle.

When Simba saw me, he was surprised. "Who are you?"

"The question is: Who are you?"

" I thought I knew. Now I'm not so sure."

"Well, I know who you are. You're Mufasa's boy. He's alive, and I'll show him to you. You follow old Rafiki. He knows the way."

I led Simba to a reflecting pool. When he looked into the water, he saw a lion. "That's not my father. It's just my reflection."

"No, look harder…You see, he lives in you."

The ghost of Mufasa magically appeared. "Look inside yourself, Simba. You are more than what you have become. You must take your place in the Circle of Life."

Encouraged by his father's words, Simba returned to Pride Rock. Nala, Pumbaa, and Timon followed. When Simba arrived, he found the land bare and dry. The hyenas were in control, and Scar was shouting at Simba's mother. Sarabi turned to Scar.

"We must leave Pride Rock."

"We're not going anywhere. I am the king."

"If you were half the king Mufasa was—"

"I AM TEN TIMES THE KING MUFASA WAS!"

Suddenly a flash of lightning revealed the edge of Pride Rock, and there stood Simba. Scar jumped back.

"Simba...I'm a little surprised to see you...alive."

"Give me one good reason why I shouldn't rip you apart."

But Scar forced Simba to say, in front of all the lions, that he had caused his father's death.

Scar smirked. "Oh Simba, you're in trouble again. But this time Daddy isn't here to save you. And now everyone knows why."

Simba backed up against the ledge. Lightning struck again, setting fire to the dry brush of the Pride Lands.

Simba, knowing the truth, leapt on Scar. Nala and the other lionesses joined the battle. Through the smoke and flames of the brushfire, Simba spotted Scar trying to escape and he ran after the old lion. Scar pleaded with his nephew.

"Simba, I'll make it up to you. I promise. And how can I prove myself to you?"

"Run. Run away, Scar, and never return."

Scar started to slink off, but then he turned and lunged one last time at Simba. Simba moved quickly and flipped Scar over the ledge, where a pack of hyenas were waiting hungrily.

Limping badly, Simba climbed up to the very top of Pride Rock. He let out a magnificent roar as he looked out over his kingdom.

Before long, Pride Rock flourished again. Nala remained by Simba's side, and soon they had their own newborn cub. With all their friends around, including Zazu, Pumbaa and Timon, a new celebration of life took place. After making a mark over the forehead of the young cub, I held him up for all the kingdom to see.